SMALL WORLD

WORDS BY ISHTA MERCURIO
PICTURES BY JEN CORACE

ABRAMS BOOKS FOR YOUNG READERS, NEW YORK

When Nanda was born,
the whole of the world was
wrapped in the circle of her
mother's arms:

safe,
warm,
small.

But as she grew,
the world grew, too.

It became the circle of
her loving family...

A bubble of giggling playmates . . .

And slides and swings and whirligigs and tumbles through the grass.

Nanda got bigger and bigger. But as she grew, the world grew, too.

It became a sway of branches . . .

Scaffolds of steel . . .

And cables

and cogs

and odds

and sods

and coasting through
the night.

Nanda got bigger
and even bigger.
But as she
grew, the
world grew,
too.

It became a sun-kissed maze of wheat...

Pinecone-prickled mountains and the microscopic elegance of fractals in the snow.

It soared through a symphony of glass and stone.

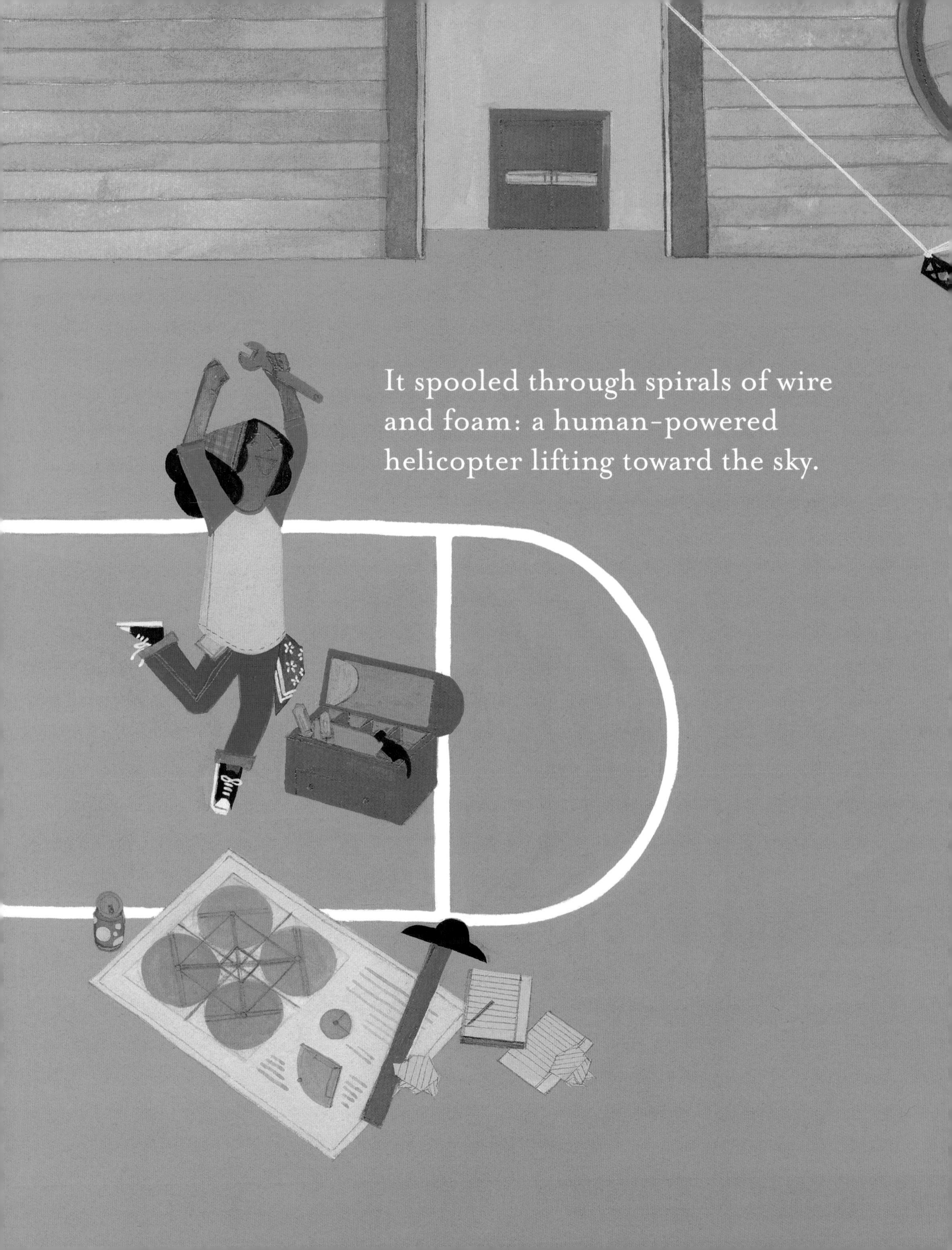

It spooled through spirals of wire and foam: a human-powered helicopter lifting toward the sky.

Nanda got bigger and
bigger and BIGGER.
But as she grew, the
world grew, too.

It became the roar of twin engines, a glittering ocean far below, and the curve of the planet beneath her.

On a day when Nanda was bigger than she had ever been before, her feet touched foreign soil.

Her ears heard a crackle of voices.
She gazed out into ink-black space
and saw . . .

A sea of stars, moonless and deep,
distant suns twinkling...

Marbled planets orbiting,
speck-small in the distant
night...

And the Earth, softly glowing.
A circle called home:

safe,
and warm,
and small.

For A and C, who grow my world a little more every day
—I. M.

For Iris Naomi
—J. C.

AUTHOR'S NOTE

Earth is shaped like a huge ball. It's so huge that to someone standing on Earth, it doesn't seem like a ball at all. To see the ball shape, you have to go into space. But from space, it *doesn't* look huge. That's because even though the Earth is really, really big, the universe is many, many times bigger. When you go out into space, it's easier to see how small the Earth is compared to the size of the universe.

You can think of Earth as being both big and small at the same time in the same way that you are big and small at the same time. You are smaller than your parents, but bigger than a pinecone or a snowflake. And you have big ideas! Just like Nanda, if you stick with your ideas as you grow older, you will see more of our world and maybe even more of the universe.

Nanda travels to many places in this book. If you were Nanda, where would *you* go? What places have you visited already? Picture the world. What does it look like to you? What do you *want* the world to look like?

ABOUT NANDA'S NAME

When the time came to name the girl in this book, I kept thinking about a picture I had seen of five women at the Indian Space Research Organization celebrating after they had helped put a satellite into orbit around Mars. The photograph spoke to girls all over the world. It said, "*You* can do this." In honor of these women and their work, I named the girl in my story Nanda, which means "joy."

The art for this book was created with gouache, ink, and pencil on Rives BFK.

Library of Congress Cataloging-in-Publication Data

Names: Mercurio, Ishta, author. | Corace, Jen, illustrator.
Title: Small world / by Ishta Mercurio; illustrations, Jen Corace.
Description: New York: Abrams Books for Young Readers, 2019. | Summary:
First, Nanda's entire world is the circle of her mother's arms but as she
grows, she sees the wonder of whirligigs, fractals in the snow, and even
the circle of the Earth, itself.
Identifiers: LCCN 2018009608 | ISBN 9781419734076 (hardcover with jacket)
Subjects: | CYAC: Wonder—Fiction.
Classification: LCC PZ7.1.M4755 Sm 2019 | DDC [E]—dc23

Book design by Chad W. Beckerman

Printed and bound in China
10 9 8 7 6 5 4 3 2 1

ABRAMS The Art of Books
195 Broadway, New York, NY 10007
abramsbooks.com

DiMaggio was the greatest all-round player I saw. . . . But Joe DiMaggio's career cannot be summed up in numbers and awards. It might sound corny, but he had a profound and lasting impact on the country.

—Ted Williams, left fielder,
Boston Red Sox

THE STREAK

HOW JOE DIMAGGIO BECAME AMERICA'S HERO

Barb Rosenstock
Illustrated by
Terry Widener

CALKINS CREEK
AN IMPRINT OF HIGHLIGHTS
Honesdale, Pennsylvania

I'm just a ball player with one ambition, and that is to give all I've got to help my ball club win. I've never played any other way.

—Joe DiMaggio, center fielder,
New York Yankees

TALK OF U.S.
NTERING
HE FIGHT

It all started quietly, like a conversation with Joe DiMaggio himself.

One shy single, hit to left field,

smack in the middle of May, the fifteenth.

The Yankees, Joe's team, lost 13 to 1. It wasn't news. Instead, the headlines in 1941 shouted about the war spreading like a fever through Europe. No one knew it, but that one hit was something special—the start of the most perfect summer in baseball.

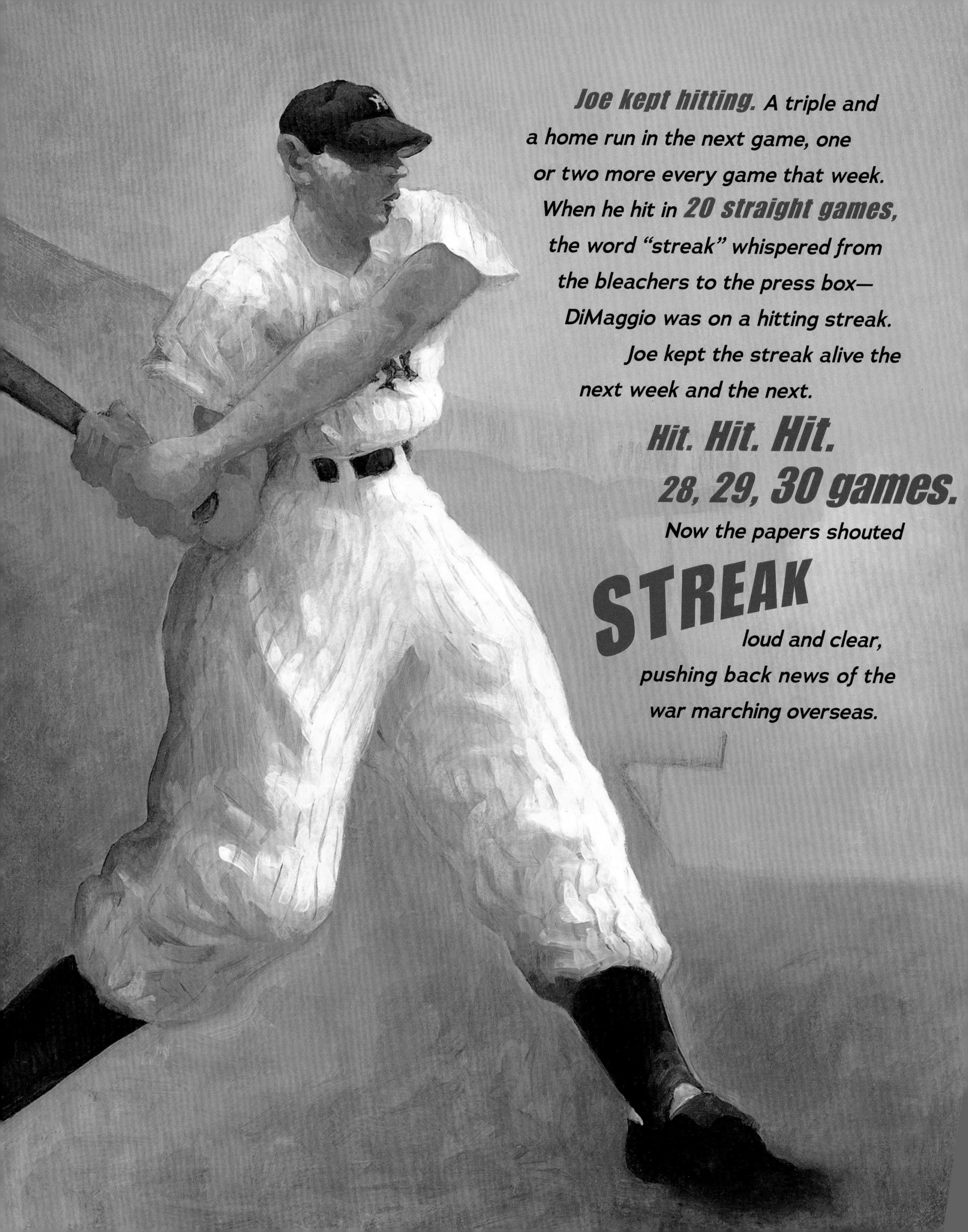

Joe kept hitting. *A triple and a home run in the next game, one or two more every game that week. When he hit in* ***20 straight games,*** *the word "streak" whispered from the bleachers to the press box—DiMaggio was on a hitting streak. Joe kept the streak alive the next week and the next.*

Hit. Hit. Hit.

28, 29, 30 games.

Now the papers shouted

STREAK

loud and clear, pushing back news of the war marching overseas.

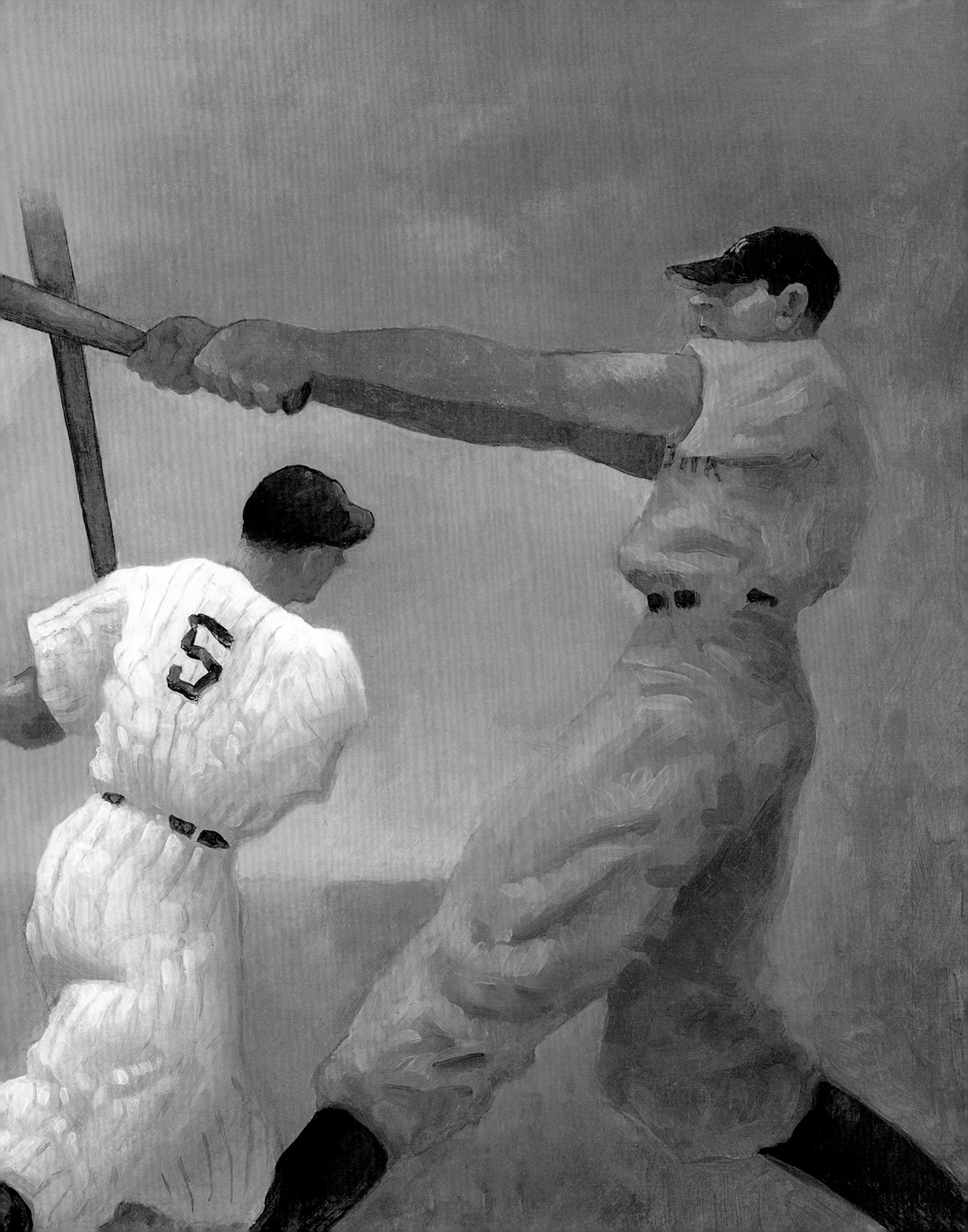
5

DiMaggio wasn't like Ruth, Cobb, or Foxx. He was a boy with a funny-sounding name, part of the crowd of American kids whose parents came from another country, didn't speak English, and worked till they dropped. Joe grew up on the San Francisco wharf, the eighth of nine children in a fisherman's family. He scrubbed decks, fixed torn nets, and hawked newspapers to help feed them. His hands knew hard work. Now, wrapped around a bat, they were the most famous hands in America.

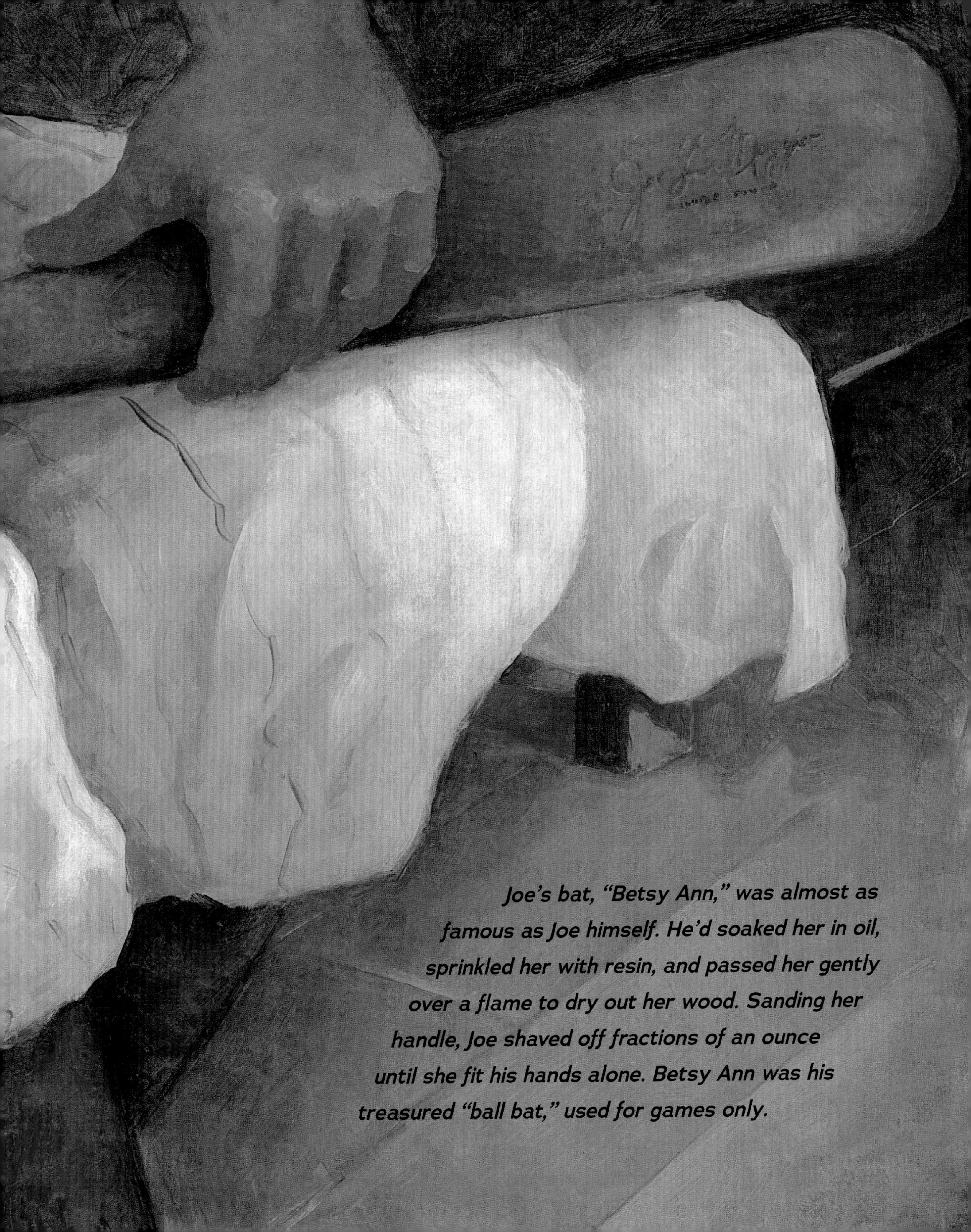

Joe's bat, "Betsy Ann," was almost as famous as Joe himself. He'd soaked her in oil, sprinkled her with resin, and passed her gently over a flame to dry out her wood. Sanding her handle, Joe shaved off fractions of an ounce until she fit his hands alone. Betsy Ann was his treasured "ball bat," used for games only.

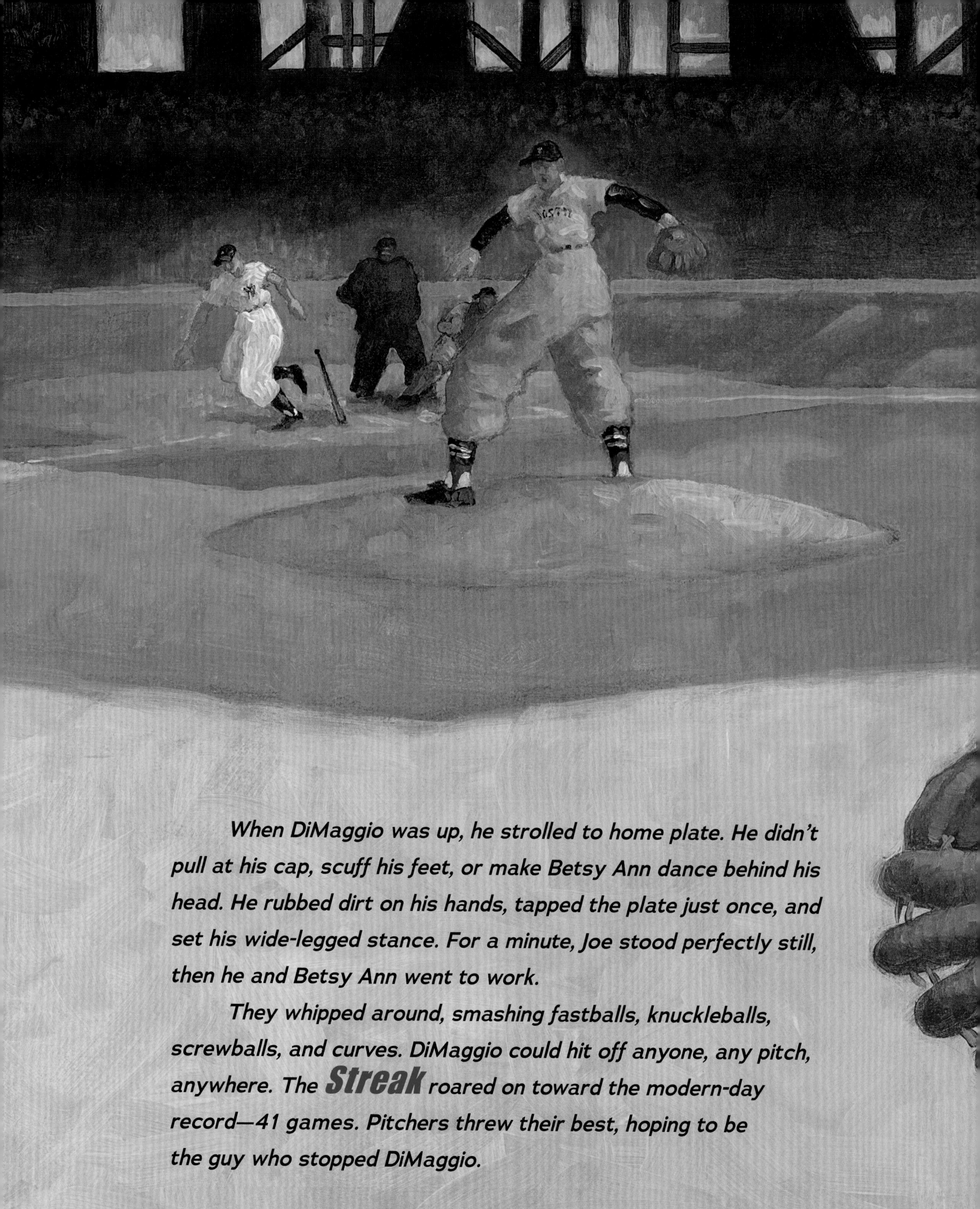

When DiMaggio was up, he strolled to home plate. He didn't pull at his cap, scuff his feet, or make Betsy Ann dance behind his head. He rubbed dirt on his hands, tapped the plate just once, and set his wide-legged stance. For a minute, Joe stood perfectly still, then he and Betsy Ann went to work.

They whipped around, smashing fastballs, knuckleballs, screwballs, and curves. DiMaggio could hit off anyone, any pitch, anywhere. The **Streak** roared on toward the modern-day record—41 games. Pitchers threw their best, hoping to be the guy who stopped DiMaggio.

On the field, Joe acted strong and confident. But off the field, he barely slept, hardly ate—his stomach hurt all the time. Keeping the Streak alive was the hardest work he'd ever done.

That summer, the crack of Joe's bat mixed with the swing-band rhythms on the radio and the drumbeats of the world at war.

Streak. Streak. Streak.

America pulled for Joe, prayed for Joe. This was the United States of Baseball and Joe DiMaggio was its President.

DIMAGGIO

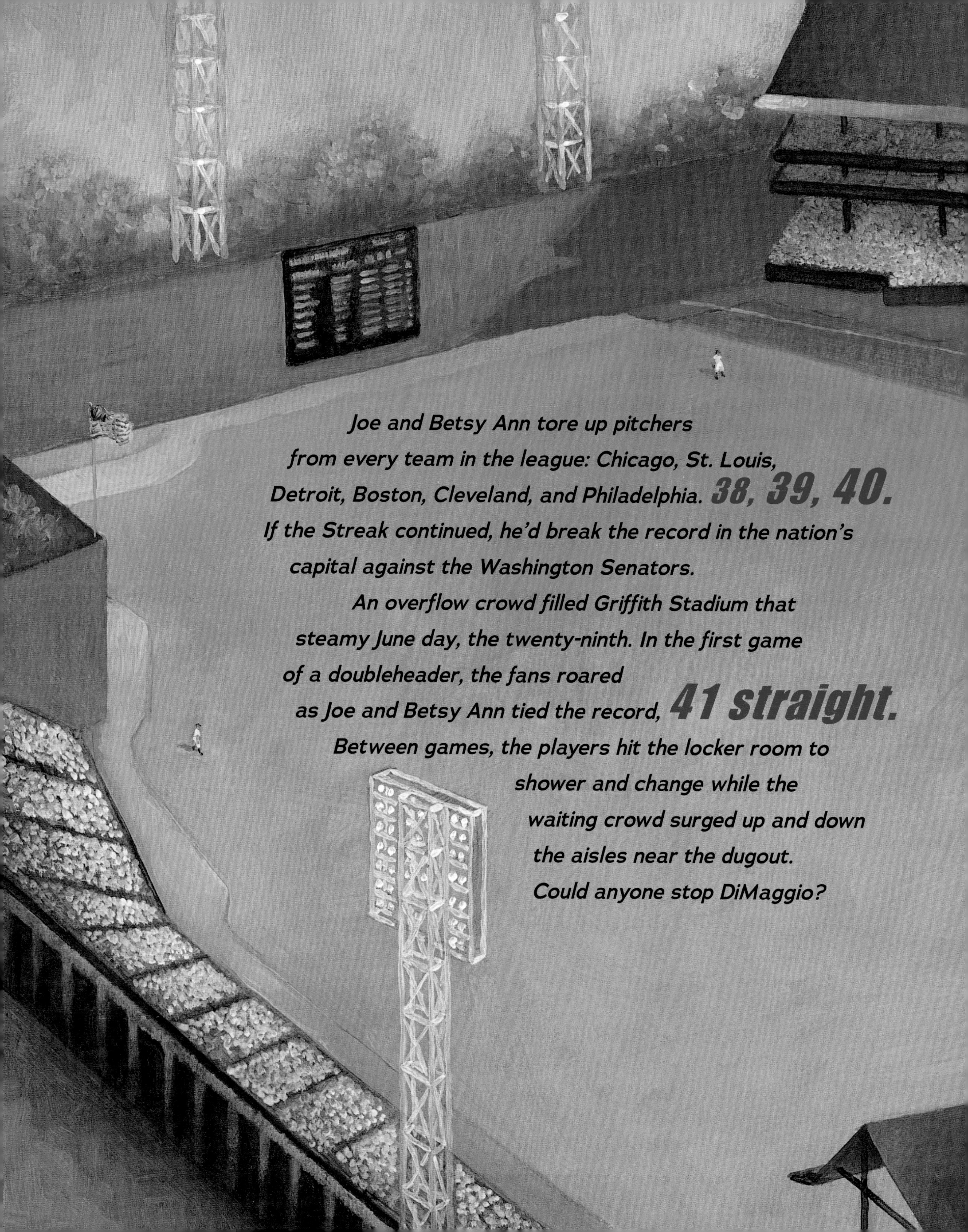

Joe and Betsy Ann tore up pitchers from every team in the league: Chicago, St. Louis, Detroit, Boston, Cleveland, and Philadelphia. **38, 39, 40.** *If the Streak continued, he'd break the record in the nation's capital against the Washington Senators.*

An overflow crowd filled Griffith Stadium that steamy June day, the twenty-ninth. In the first game of a doubleheader, the fans roared as Joe and Betsy Ann tied the record, **41 straight.** *Between games, the players hit the locker room to shower and change while the waiting crowd surged up and down the aisles near the dugout. Could anyone stop DiMaggio?*

The second game started. As always, DiMaggio batted cleanup.

In the dugout, he reached for Betsy Ann.

She was gone.

Joe yelled, "Tom! You got my ball bat!" as right fielder Tommy Henrich, batting second, trotted toward the box. DiMaggio ran over, looked at the bat in Tommy's hands. It wasn't Betsy Ann.

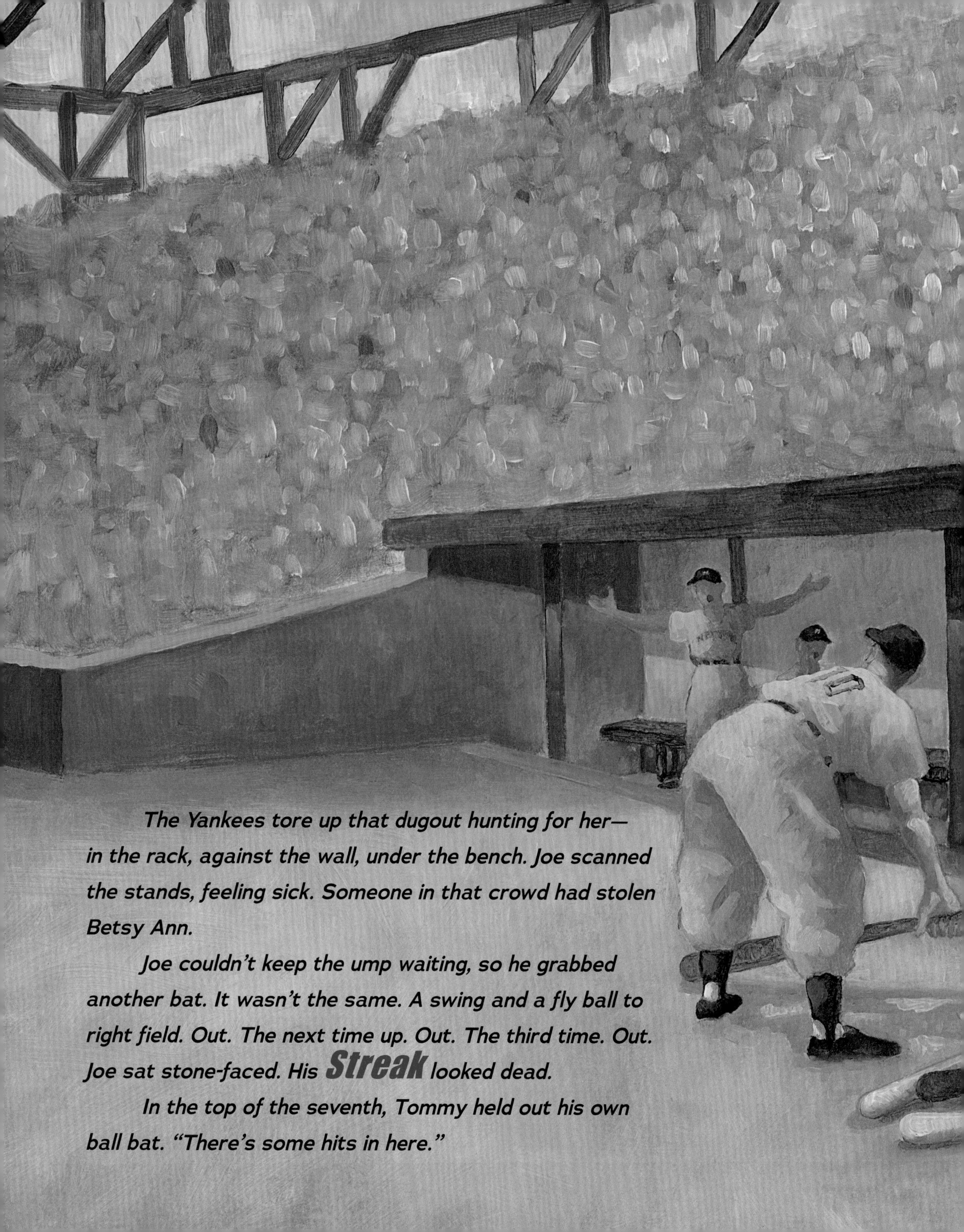

The Yankees tore up that dugout hunting for her—in the rack, against the wall, under the bench. Joe scanned the stands, feeling sick. Someone in that crowd had stolen Betsy Ann.

Joe couldn't keep the ump waiting, so he grabbed another bat. It wasn't the same. A swing and a fly ball to right field. Out. The next time up. Out. The third time. Out. Joe sat stone-faced. His **Streak** *looked dead.*

In the top of the seventh, Tommy held out his own ball bat. "There's some hits in here."

Joe grabbed Tommy's bat.
This might be his final chance.
Could he keep the **Streak** alive
without Betsy Ann? Joe wasn't sure.
DiMaggio strolled up to home plate.
He rubbed dirt on his hands,
tapped the plate just once,
and set his wide-legged stance.
Watched by thirty-one thousand
breathless fans, he stood in that
batter's box missing Betsy Ann,
and went to work anyway.

NEW YORK

On the second toss, the pitcher let a waist-high fastball fly right over the middle of the plate. Joe whacked a line drive past the left fielder's glove. Stomping screams shook the stands. No one could stop DiMaggio. No one.

Joe passed first base on his way to second, but the wild cheers got him. He tipped his cap, flickered a smile, and trotted weak-kneed back to first. The first base coach patted his back; even the Senators' first baseman shook his hand! The Yankees pounded their bats and danced up and down the dugout steps as kids scampered out of the stands and onto the field toward their hero,

America's hero, Joe DiMaggio.

Afterword

A week later, some guys found Betsy Ann in New Jersey and got her back to Joe. His hitting streak went on and on with Betsy Ann and, when she broke, without her.

5 more games. 10 more.
Joe didn't stop till he hit 56.

Riding high on the Streak, the Yankees won the 1941 World Series.

After that one perfect summer, World War II arrived, and everything, even baseball, became a part of it. America had spent the summer watching sureness and strength win against impossible odds. The country learned to pull together and celebrate together. It was ready to go to work. Joe DiMaggio showed the way.

#1: Joe DiMaggio's 56-Game Hitting Streak

—"Sports Greatest Records,"
Sporting News, 2011

Author's Note

Joe DiMaggio's 56-game hitting streak has been called "the record that will never be broken." Though DiMaggio was uncomfortable with publicity, that summer of 1941 his name was in every newspaper, fans mobbed him on the street, and bulletins of his hitting progress interrupted programming on the radio. The person who stole Joe's ball bat "Betsy Ann" has never been identified. By July 7, Betsy Ann was returned to DiMaggio in New York, and he began using her again. On July 23, sports columnist Harry Grayson reported that Betsy Ann broke as DiMaggio hit a lazy pop fly in a game against the Chicago White Sox on July 14, game 54 of the Streak. As always, if Joe was upset, he didn't seem to show it. Grayson wrote, "DiMaggio took the loss of his pet stick like he took the cracking of his amazing batting skein—all in stride."

Though sports equipment factories make bats to the specifications of major leaguers, players today still alter their bats within the rules to get the feel just right. In the past, bats have been rubbed with manure, chewing tobacco, and paraffin wax. Today, some players smear the handle with pine tar or wind tape around it to give them a better grip. They rub the barrel on a bone, a locker, a desk, or a glass bottle to compact the wood grain. Players still use different bats for games and practice. Some still name their special bats. Major leaguers are careful, even superstitious, about how they treat their "gamers." Players have been known to sleep with a lucky bat when they are hitting well.

Hitting a baseball thrown by a professional pitcher is widely considered the single hardest activity in sports. A long hitting streak is unusual because it requires a batter to perform under intense pressure, every game, for weeks and weeks, while baseball's best pitchers try to stop him. Yet the Streak of 1941 was not DiMaggio's longest hitting streak. He holds the number 2 spot in the minor-league record books with a 61-game streak set with the San Francisco Seals of the Pacific Coast League when he was eighteen years old. The minor-league record holder is Joe Wilhoit, who in 1919 hit in an incredible 69 straight games for the Wichita Witches of the Western League.

Before 1941, the modern-day streak record of 41 games was held by first baseman George Sisler of the St. Louis Browns in the American League. As Joe DiMaggio's 1941 hitting streak moved forward, a reporter dug up an even older record: 44 consecutive games in a single season by Baltimore Orioles outfielder Willie Keeler way back in 1897, before foul balls were counted as strikes. On July 2, DiMaggio smashed Keeler's mark, too, on his way to the final number of 56 straight games.

The Streak ended on July 17, 1941, against pitchers Al Smith and Jim Bagby of the Cleveland Indians, who held Joe hitless thanks to two whacks both stopped by third baseman Ken Keltner. For the first putout, Keltner made a difficult backhanded play. Statisticians and probability experts have estimated that a streak like DiMaggio's could occur once every 746 to 18,519 years—in other words, it was practically impossible. Though DiMaggio's record hasn't been bested so far, in baseball, as in life, there is always surprise, opportunity, and hope. There are five other Major League players who've hit in 40 or more games, but no one has come within 10 games of DiMaggio, and no one's performance in baseball has meant more at the time to the country.

In December 1941, the United States officially entered World War II when Japan bombed Pearl Harbor in Hawaii. Baseball became part of the war effort. For the morale of the country, President Franklin D. Roosevelt instructed Major League Baseball to continue the 1942 baseball season. Hillerich & Bradsby, the famous manufacturer of Louisville Slugger bats, transformed its factory to produce wooden rifle stocks. And sixteen Major League teams saw more than five hundred players enter military service, either through enlistment or the draft. In 1941, baseball was six years away from integration by Jackie Robinson. However, Negro League players joined the armed forces in large numbers to serve a country that didn't treat them as equal citizens. Many players, DiMaggio included, gave up the best years of their baseball careers to serve their country.

That's one record I've wanted to crack ever since I came up in the major leagues.

—Joe DiMaggio

Congratulations. I'm glad a real hitter broke it.

—George Sisler, first baseman, St. Louis Browns, and previous streak record holder

Joe DiMaggio boomed his way into baseball's row of immortals.

—Associated Press

Top-Ten Major League Baseball Hitting Streaks

56 games: Joe DiMaggio, 1941
45 games: Willie Keeler, 1896–1897
44 games: Pete Rose, 1978
42 games: Bill Dahlen, 1894
41 games: George Sisler, 1922
40 games: Ty Cobb, 1911
39 games: Paul Molitor, 1987
38 games: Jimmy Rollins, 2005–2006
37 games: Tommy Holmes, 1945
36 games: Gene DeMontreville, 1896–1897

The current MLB practice is to total hitting streaks over two consecutive seasons. Keeler's current total is 45 hits (1896–97 seasons), but in 1941 his record was counted as a single season total of 44.

DiMaggio's Streak Statistics, May 15–July 16, 1941

G	AB	R	H	2B	3B	HR	RBI	BB	AVG.	SLG.
56	223	56	91	16	4	15	55	21	.408	.717

DiMaggio's 1941 Regular-Season Statistics

G	AB	R	H	2B	3B	HR	RBI	BB	AVG.	SLG.
139	541	122	193	43	11	30	125*	76	.357	.643

**Led American League*

DiMaggio's Lifetime Statistics (13-Year Career)

G	AB	R	H	2B	3B	HR	RBI	BB	AVG.	SLG.
1,736	6,821	1,390	2,214	389	131	361	1,537	790	.325	.579

Sources for stats: MLB.com, baseball-almanac.com, and baseball-reference.com

Source Notes*

Each citation indicates the first words of the quotation and its document source. Most of the sources are listed in the bibliography. Sources are provided below for those not included in the bibliography. Every effort has been made to trace and identify the ownership of the following text quotations.

Front endpaper

"DiMaggio was . . .": Williams, *Ted Williams' Hit List* by Ted Williams and Jim Prime. Indianapolis: Masters Press, 1996, p. 79.

Page 2

"I'm just a . . .": DiMaggio, quoted in Bannon and Wright, p. 24.

Page 19

"Tom! You got . . .": Henrich, quoted in "Joe DiMaggio: The Hero's Life." PBS, *The American Experience*, 2000, pbs.org/wgbh/amex/dimaggio/filmmore/reference/interview/heinrich04.html.

Page 20

"There's some hits . . .": Henrich, quoted in Vaccaro, p. 176.

Page 28

"#1: Joe DiMaggio's . . .": Crossman, Fagan, et al., p. 16.

"DiMaggio took the . . .": Grayson, p. 2.

Page 29

"That's one record . . .": DiMaggio, quoted in Magruder, p. 17.

"Congratulations. I'm glad . . .": Sisler, quoted in *San Antonio Light* (International News Service), p. 6A.

"Joe DiMaggio boomed . . .": Associated Press, p. 10.

Back endpaper

"He would be . . .": Cobb, quoted in Bannon and Wright, p. 54.

Newspaper Headlines

The newspaper headlines that appear in the illustrations on pages 4–5, 14–15, and 26–27 are courtesy of *Bismarck Tribune*, Bismarck, North Dakota; *Lock Haven Express*, Lock Haven, Pennsylvania; *Fairbanks Daily News-Minor*, Fairbanks, Alaska; and *Mason City Globe*, Mason City, Iowa.

Bibliography*

Books

Allen, Maury. *Where Have You Gone, Joe DiMaggio?: The Story of America's Last Hero.* New York: E. P. Dutton, 1975.

Bannon, Joseph J., and Joanna L. Wright, coor. eds. *Joe DiMaggio: An American Icon.* Daily News Legends Series. Champaign, IL: Sports Publishing, 2000.

Cramer, Richard Ben. *Joe DiMaggio: The Hero's Life.* New York: Simon and Schuster, 2000.

DiMaggio, Joe, and Richard Whittingham. *The DiMaggio Albums.* Vols. 1 and 2. New York: Putnam, 1989.

Durso, Joseph. *DiMaggio: The Last American Knight.* Boston: Little, Brown, 1995.

Johnson, Dick, and Glenn Stout. *DiMaggio: An Illustrated Life.* New York: Walker and Company, 1995.

Kennedy, Kostya. *56: Joe DiMaggio and the Last Magic Number in Sports.* New York: Time Home Entertainment, 2012.

Seidel, Michael. *Streak: Joe DiMaggio and the Summer of '41.* New York: McGraw-Hill, 1988.

Vaccaro, Mike. *1941—The Greatest Year in Sports.* New York: Doubleday, 2007.

Articles

Anderson, Dave. "The Longest Hitting Streak in History." *Sports Illustrated,* July 17, 1961.

Associated Press. "Joe DiMaggio Breaks Batting Record." *Zanesville* (OH) *Times Recorder,* June 30, 1941.

Busch, Noel F. "Close-up: Joe DiMaggio; Baseball's Most Sensational Big-League Star Starts What Should Be His Best Year So Far." *Life,* May 1, 1939.

Chass, Murray. "Amid Crumbling Records, a Streak That Will Endure." *New York Times,* March 9, 1999.

Chicago Tribune. "DiMaggio Nears New Record, as Yanks Win 7–4." June 29, 1941.

Chicago Tribune. "Joe DiMaggio Sets Modern Batting Record." June 30, 1941.

Crossman, Matt, Ryan Fagan, et al. "Sports Greatest Records." *Sporting News,* April 25, 2011.

Daley, Arthur. "14 Hits Overpower M'Carthymen, 13–1." *New York Times,* May 16, 1941.

Daniel, Dan. "Inside Joe DiMaggio." *Baseball Magazine,* February 1952.

———. "Viva Italia." *Baseball Magazine,* 1936.

Dawson, James P. "Yankees Conquer Senators, 9–4, 7–5." *New York Times*, June 30, 1941.

———. "Yanks Triumph 7–4, Retake 1st Place; Streaks Extended." *New York Times*, June 29, 1941.

Donovan, John. "Stubborn Streak." *Sports Illustrated*, June 19, 2003. si.com.

Effrat, Louis. "DiMaggio's Streak Reaches 30 Games." *New York Times*, June 18, 1941.

Evening Bulletin-Philadelphia. "DiMaggio Breaks Batting Record as Yanks Win." June 30, 1941.

Frick, Ford C. "Marks That Will Never Be Broken." Baseball Almanac. baseball-almanac.com/legendary/lifrick.shtml.

Goren, Herb. "DiMaggio Talks about His Streak." *Baseball Digest*, October 1969.

Grayson, Harry. "The Scoreboard." NEA News Service in *Biloxi Daily Herald*, July 22, 1941.

Kennedy, Kostya. "The Streak." *Sports Illustrated*, March 14, 2011. si.com.

Kirksey, George. "New Bambino! New York Tacks Ruth's Old Nickname on Slugging Di Maggio." *Chronicle Sporting Green* (UP News), July 11, 1937. sfmuseum.net/hist10/dimaggio2.html.

Magruder, Milton. "DiMaggio Isn't Satisfied; He's Out for More of 'Em." *Oakland Tribune* (UP News), June 30, 1941.

McCann, Dick. "Cobb Pulling for DiMag to Break Sisler's Mark." *New York Daily News*, June 24, 1941.

———. "DiMag Seeking Hits—Not Record Setting Streak." *New York Daily News*, June 25, 1941.

McClean, Tony. "They Chose to Serve." Black Athlete Sports Network. blackathlete.net/2006/05/they-chose-to-serve.

Neal, LaVelle E. "Pine Tar and Superstition: The Life of a Baseball Bat." *Minneapolis-St. Paul Star Tribune*, May 17, 2007.

Owen, Russell. "DiMaggio, the Unruffled." *New York Times*, July 13, 1941.

San Antonio Light. "Sisler's Mark His, DiMag Sets Sail for Keeler's" (International News Service). June 30, 1941.

United Press. "Fans Steal Bats to Hamper DiMaggio in Sunday Batting." *Racine* (WI) *Journal Times*, June 30, 1941.

Washington Post. "Fans Come from Miles Around to See DiMaggio Make History." June 29, 1941.

Zimmerman, Bill. "At Least Bat-Stealers Can't Take Joe's Record." *San Antonio Light*, June 30, 1941.

Websites*

Baseball Almanac. baseball-almanac.com

Baseball-Reference.com. baseball-reference.com

Gary Bedingfield's Baseball in Wartime. baseballinwartime.com

National Baseball Hall of Fame and Museum. baseballhall.org

Additional Sources

Burns, Ken, and Geoffrey C. Ward. *Baseball*. "Inning 5: Shadow Ball" and "Inning 6: The National Pastime (1940–1950)." PBS Home Video, 1994. DVD.

Kennedy, Kostya, and Joseph M. Lavine. *Where Have You Gone, Joe DiMaggio?* New York: HBO, 1997. DVD.

National Baseball Hall of Fame and Museum, Cooperstown, New York. Author's visit, August 2008.

Acknowledgments

I discovered the story of Joe DiMaggio and his bat Betsy Ann on a family trip to the "Birthplace of Baseball," Cooperstown, New York, and was excited to work with the National Baseball Hall of Fame and Museum on this book.

Thanks to Gabriel Schechter, baseball researcher extraordinaire; Dave Kaplan, director of the Yogi Berra Museum and Learning Center; P. J. Shelley, tour and programming director at the Louisville Slugger Museum and Factory; Cassidy Lent, Frank and Peggy Steele Intern, and Tim Wiles, director of research, both of the National Baseball Hall of Fame and Museum, for their assistance, fact-checking, and general baseball smarts.

—*BR*

Thanks to Carolyn P. Yoder and Juanita Galuska of Calkins Creek for the hours and days they spent on the finishing touches.

—*TW*

* *Websites active at time of publication*

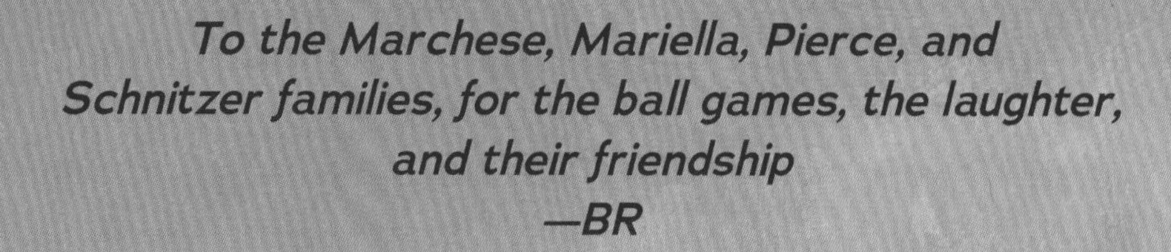

To the Marchese, Mariella, Pierce, and Schnitzer families, for the ball games, the laughter, and their friendship
—BR

To LSW (37) and the kids
—TW

Calkins Creek
An Imprint of Highlights
815 Church Street
Honesdale, Pennsylvania 18431
Printed in China

ISBN: 978-1-59078-992-6
Library of Congress Control Number: 2013947717
First edition

10 9 8 7 6 5 4 3 2 1

Designed by Barbara Grzeslo
Production by Margaret Mosomillo
The text is set in Adrianna Italic and Impact.
The illustrations are done in acrylic on bristol paper.

He would be a great star at any time in the history of the game. He is one of the greatest hitters, quickest fielders, surest throwers, and fastest runners I've seen.

—Ty Cobb, outfielder,
Detroit Tigers